Each One Special

*For my father, artist Chaim Reches
and my friend Vida Hofmann*
F.W.

*Mostly to my father, Daniel,
a lot to Hamish the baker from Nanaimo,
and a special thanks to Paris,
one very creative spirit on Salt Spring Island.*
H.W.Z.

Each One Special

written *by* Frieda Wishinsky
illustrated by H. Werner Zimmermann

ORCA BOOK PUBLISHERS

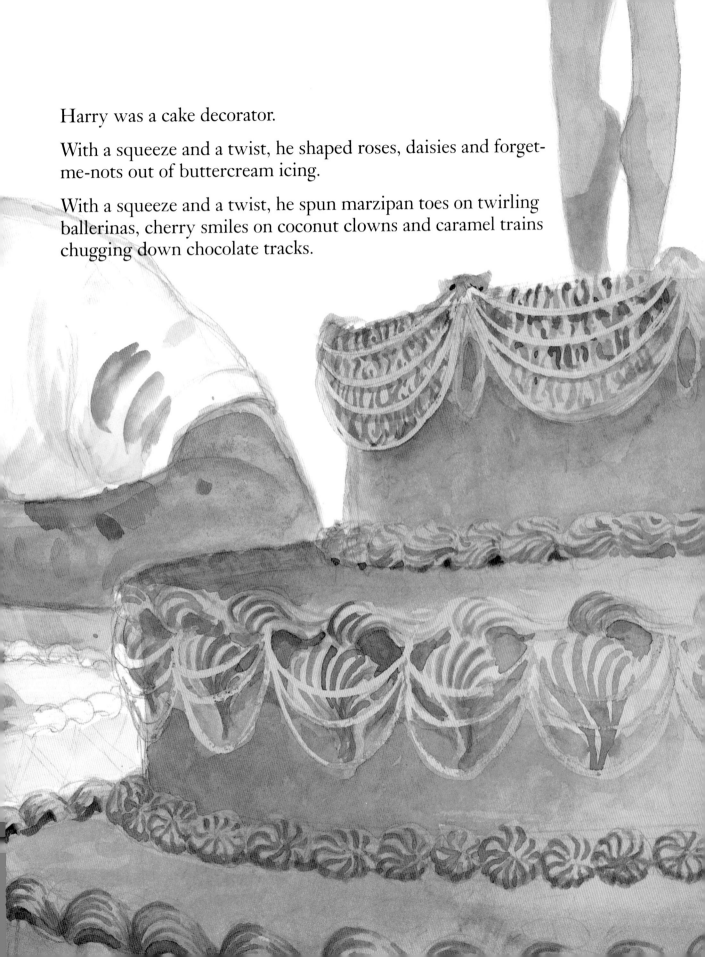

Harry was a cake decorator.

With a squeeze and a twist, he shaped roses, daisies and forget-me-nots out of buttercream icing.

With a squeeze and a twist, he spun marzipan toes on twirling ballerinas, cherry smiles on coconut clowns and caramel trains chugging down chocolate tracks.

Every day after school Ben visited Harry at the bakery.

Sometimes Harry let Ben help decorate. Sometimes Ben swirled a petal on a flower or a smile on a face.

Ben loved helping Harry. He loved watching Harry make each cake different and each cake special.

Harry's customers loved his cakes too.

"Ooh," they applauded when Harry opened the cake box.

"Ahh," they sighed as Harry turned their cake from side to side.

"A masterpiece!" they proclaimed as they carefully carried their cake home.

Each year on Ben's birthday, Harry made Ben a special cake.

One year he made a raspberry rocketship landing on a walnut moon.

Another year he made a mint racing car striped in yellow and red.

But Ben's favorite cake was the tall mocha cowboy spinning a butterscotch lasso.

"Harry," said Ben, "you can make anything!"

And Harry could.

Then one day the owner of Harry's bakery sold his shop. The new owners wanted new bakers.

"But I have thirty-five years of experience," Harry told them. "And each cake I make is different. Each cake is special."

"We want fast, not different," they told him.

"We want lots, not special," they said.

"We want young bakers, not old," they insisted.

Harry looked for a new job. But he couldn't find one.

Harry didn't know what to do.

"Go fishing," said Harry's wife Fran. But all Harry caught was a cold.

"Try golf," said Fran. But Harry hit everything except the golf ball.

"How about bowling?" said Fran. But Harry's bowling balls bounced into the wrong lane.

"Collect stamps," said Fran. But Harry liked to make things, not collect them.

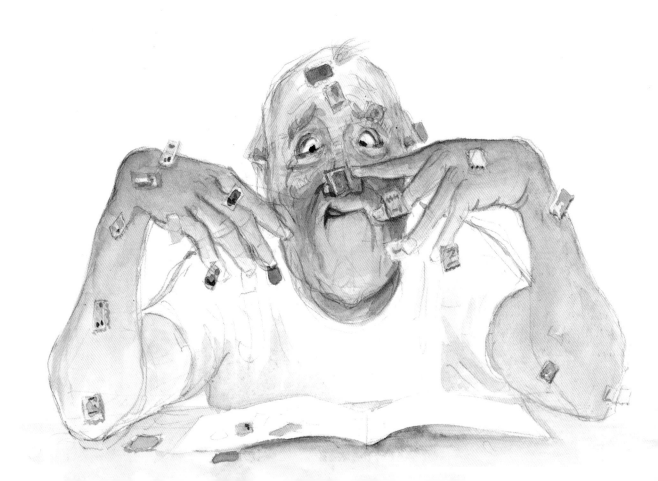

Soon all Harry did was sit in his blue chair and watch TV.

"He's not the same man," said Fran, her eyes full of tears.

"Harry is still Harry," Ben told her. "He just hasn't found what he wants to do."

But as Ben watched Harry sit in his chair, even Ben began to worry. He missed Harry's laughs as Harry shaped and squeezed. He missed Harry's smiles as customers oohed and ahhed. But most of all, he missed the old Harry.

Then one day Ben's mom bought him some clay.

Ben played with the clay. He made a bird and a cat. Then he tried to make a cowboy, but he couldn't.

So Ben took the clay over to Harry.

"Can you make a cowboy out of this clay?" he asked.

"What do I know about working with clay?" said Harry. "All I know is cakes."

"But Harry," said Ben, hugging him tight, "you can make anything!"

Harry smiled.

"All right," Harry said. "Let's have a look at your clay."

Harry picked up a handful.

He squeezed it between his fingers. He twisted it in his hands. He turned it this way and that.

Slowly, slowly a shape appeared.

"Harry!" Ben shouted. "It's a rose!"

"You're right!" said Harry. "It is!"

Harry took some more clay. He squeezed and twisted. He turned it this way and that.

"A daisy!" Ben shouted.

"Now watch this," said Harry.

In no time, a bouquet burst out of the clay.

"You're a magician, Harry," said Ben. "Now please make a cowboy!"

"A cowboy is not so easy," laughed Harry.

"But you can do it," Ben said. "I know you can."

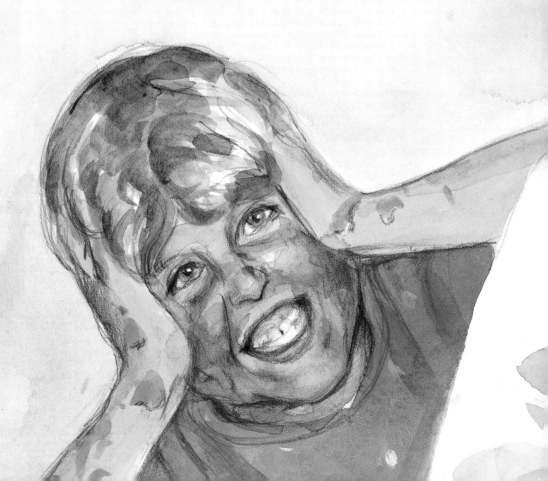

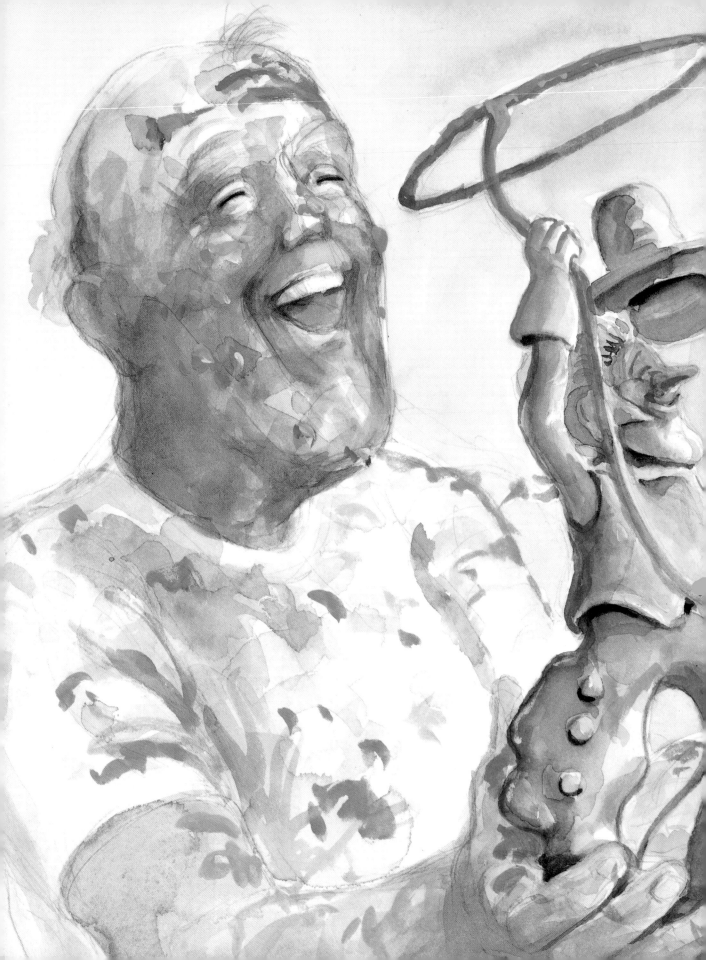

"Then let's give it a try," said Harry, and he began to shape the clay. Soon a tall cowboy popped out of the clay spinning a lasso.

"He's great!" said Ben. "But he needs a hat."

"Then give him one," said Harry, and he handed Ben a lump of clay.

Ben twisted and pulled the clay. He turned it this way and that till he shaped a tall hat. Carefully Ben placed it on the cowboy's head.

"I love it!" exclaimed Harry. "And I love this clay. It's fun. It's like buttercream icing. It's like marzipan and caramel. I'm going to buy some clay."

The next day Harry bought two big bags of clay. Soon Harry was busy twisting and shaping. Beside him, Ben twisted and shaped too.

It was not long before people came to see Harry and Ben's sculptures and to buy them. And when they arrived, Ben showed them around.

"Ooh! Ahh!" they exclaimed. "What masterpieces!"

For just like Harry's cakes...

Each sculpture was different. Each one was special.

Text copyright © 1998 Frieda Wishinsky
Illustration copyright © 1998 H. Werner Zimmermann

First paperback edition, 2001

Canadian Cataloguing in Publication Data
Wishinsky, Frieda.
Each one special

ISBN 1-55143-124-6 (pbk.)

I. Zimmermann, H. Werner (Heinz Werner), 1951–. II. Title.
PS8595.I834E32 1998   jC813'.54   C97-911109-9
PZ7.W78032Ea 1998

Library of Congress Catalog Card Number: 97-81094

Orca Book Publishers gratefully acknowledges the support of our
publishing programs provided by the following agencies: the
Department of Canadian Heritage, The Canada Council for the
Arts, and the British Columbia Arts Council.

Design by Christine Toller

Printed and bound in Hong Kong

IN CANADA:
Orca Book Publishers
PO Box 5626, Station B
Victoria, BC Canada
V8R 6S4

IN THE UNITED STATES:
Orca Book Publishers
PO Box 468
Custer, WA   USA
98240-0468

02 01 00 • 5 4 3 2 1